How the Easter Bunny Saved Christmas

For my brothers, Dave and Greg, who have spent their share of time on Santa's naughty list.
And for their wives, Regina and Linda, who are always nice.

SIMON & SCHUSTER BOOKS FOR YOUNG READERS
An imprint of Simon & Schuster Children's Publishing Division
1230 Avenue of the Americas, New York, New York 10020
Copyright © 2006 by Derek Anderson
All rights reserved, including the right of reproduction in whole or in part in any form.
SIMON & SCHUSTER BOOKS FOR YOUNG READERS is a trademark of
Simon & Schuster, Inc.
Book design by Daniel Roode
The text for this book is set in Goudy
The paintings for this book were rendered in acrylic paint, snow, and ice on wrapping
paper from Santa's Workshop.
No rabbits, reindeer, or Santas were injured during the making of this book
Manufactured in China
10 9 8 7 6 5 4 3 2 1
Library of Congress Cataloging-in-Publication Data
Anderson, Derek, 1969–
How the Easter Bunny saved Christmas / by Derek Anderson ; illustrated by Derek
Anderson.— 1st ed.
p. cm.
Summary: When Santa is unable to make his rounds, Mrs. Claus calls on the only one who
can take his place, but the reindeer have doubts about whether a half-frozen, carrot-cake
eater can handle the job.
ISBN-13: 978-0-689-87634-9
ISBN-10: 0-689-87634-3
[1. Christmas—Fiction. 2. Rabbits—Fiction. 3. Reindeer—Fiction. 4. Santa Claus—
Fiction.] I. Title.
PZ7.A53313How 2006
[E]—dc22
2005034305

NORTH POLE

How the Easter Bunny Saved Christmas

Written and illustrated by Derek Anderson

SIMON & SCHUSTER BOOKS FOR YOUNG READERS
New York   London   Toronto   Sydney

One cold, blustery Christmas Eve not long ago, Santa was helping the elves load the sleigh. He was filling the last bag of gifts when he bent down for just a second and that's when it happened.

Choo choo! POW!

A toy train bonked him right on the noodle.

It knocked him as flat as a penguin pancake!

Poor Santa was out cold.

After the doctor put Santa to bed, Mrs. Claus turned her attention to Christmas. "What are we going to do?" she cried. There was no one to deliver the gifts. Mrs. Claus had to look after Santa, the elves didn't know the route, and the entire team of reindeer was brand new. There was only one thing left to do.

Mrs. Claus called the only other fellow who makes the trip every year in one night.

"I'll be there in two shakes of a cottontail," said the Easter Bunny. And he dashed off to the snowy north to help.

The Easter Bunny climbed aboard Santa's sleigh and called the new reindeer by name, "On Flicker, on Flapper, on Jumbo and Fritz! On Rocky, on Rosie, on Lumpy and Blitz!" And the Christmas sleigh was off.

The only problem was, the Easter Bunny forgot to open the barn doors and they crashed through, nearly knocking the reindeer silly.

"Oops, sorry fellas," he said. The reindeer were not amused.

"Not even close," said Flapper.

"Just look at him," said Jumbo.

"He doesn't even like cookies. He wants carrot cake," said Fritz.

But the real trouble began when the Easter Bunny tried to follow Santa's secret notes. Every home has a special place where they like Santa to leave their presents. And the Easter Bunny just didn't understand. He did everything wrong.

Please put the Farnsworth family's gifts right under the tree.

The Meyers like their presents in their stockings.

The Watsons like their gifts placed directly under the holly.

But it wasn't until they stopped on a snowy roof in the Midwest that everything changed. The Easter Bunny was freezing his cottontail off and the deliveries were getting behind. He was trying to hurry when he took one step out of the sleigh and slipped off the roof into a giant snowbank below.

When the reindeer looked over the edge, they saw the Easter Bunny lying in a perfectly Santa-shaped hole. And they suddenly saw him like they never had before.

"You know, he isn't trying to take the place of Santa," said Rocky.

"He's just filling in," said Rosie.

"He'll need help if he wants to save Christmas," said Lumpy.

"Let's jingle," said Blitz.

After pulling the Easter Bunny from the snowbank,
Flicker, Flapper, Jumbo and Fritz, Rocky, Rosie, Lumpy
and Blitz bounced onto the sleigh.

Each grabbed a bag of gifts and, one by one,
they flew off to homes across the neighborhood.

"Merry Christmas to all!" cried the Easter Bunny. And suddenly he wasn't cold anymore. Slipping in and out of snow-capped chimneys, the Easter Bunny and reindeer quickly caught up. They worked together delivering to every home and apartment, every condo, cabin, and camper in the world until they'd finished the entire list.

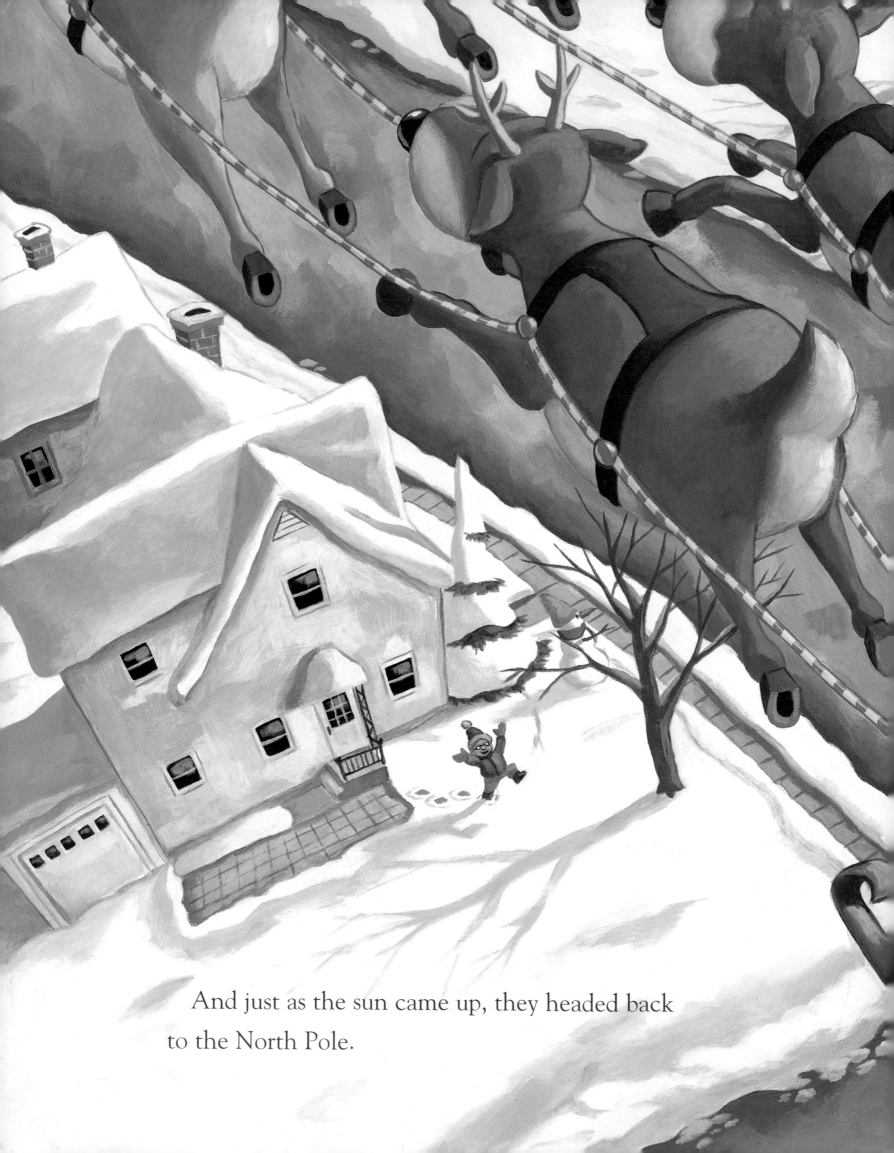

And just as the sun came up, they headed back to the North Pole.

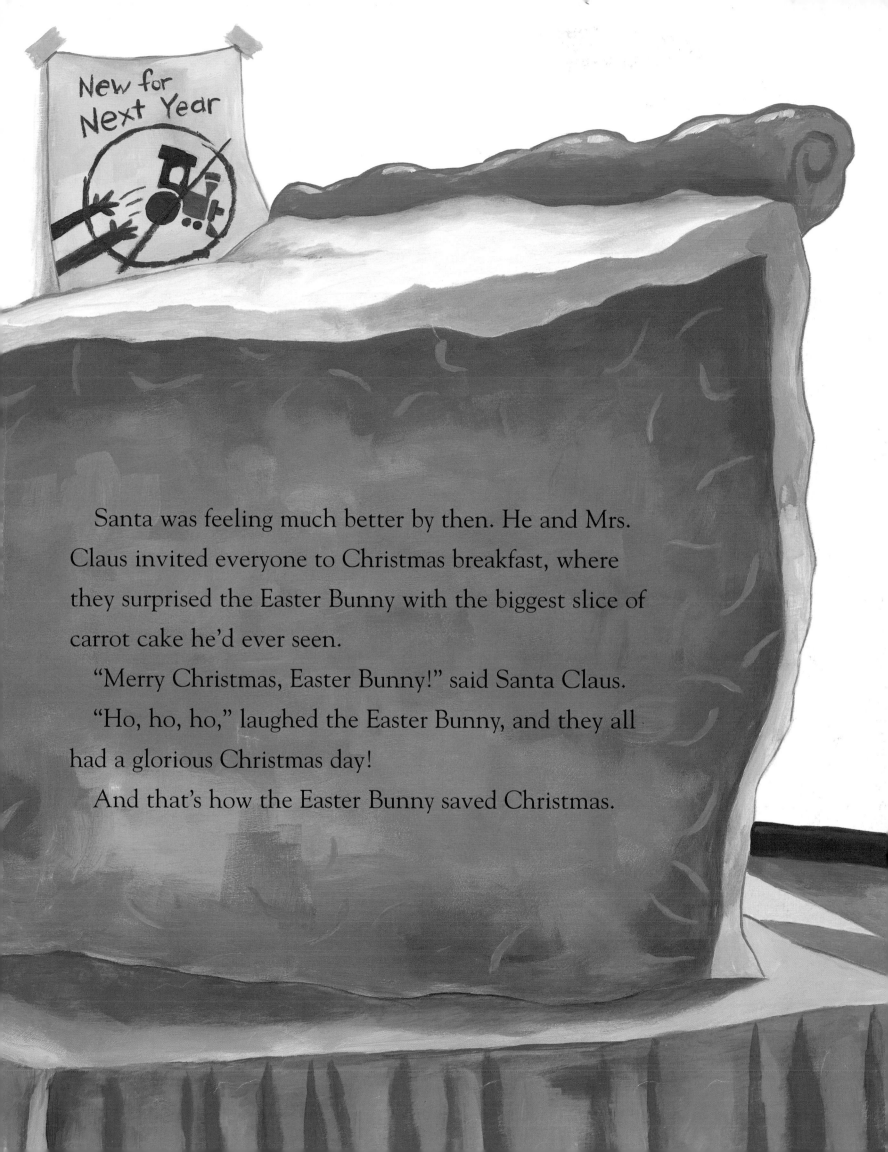

Santa was feeling much better by then. He and Mrs. Claus invited everyone to Christmas breakfast, where they surprised the Easter Bunny with the biggest slice of carrot cake he'd ever seen.

"Merry Christmas, Easter Bunny!" said Santa Claus.

"Ho, ho, ho," laughed the Easter Bunny, and they all had a glorious Christmas day!

And that's how the Easter Bunny saved Christmas.

Well, sort of.